Gracie

Doesn't
Care

Written and Illustrated by
Ruthann Cramer

For all the primary
caregivers that love
a child who is venturing
to overcome autism.

This is Zachery.
Somebody said he has
autism.

But Gracie doesn't care.

Somebody said that Zachery doesn't play with other children.

But Gracie doesn't care.

Somebody said that Zachery sings the same song over and over and over again.

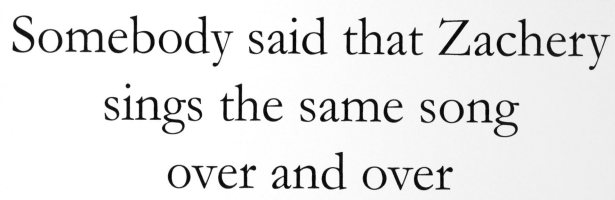

OOOOWWW!

But Gracie doesn't care.

And Somebody said that
Zachery has to eat
gluten free food.

But Gracie doesn't care.

Somebody said that Zachery always runs in circles.

But Gracie doesn't care.

Somebody said Zachery likes pirates and shapes
which he always says in the same order.

Rectangle, triangle, circle, square,

rectangle, triangle, circle, square...

Rectangle

Triangle

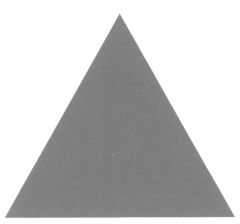

Circle

Square

But

Gracie

doesn't

care.

Somebody said that Zachery can't sleep at night.

But Gracie doesn't care.

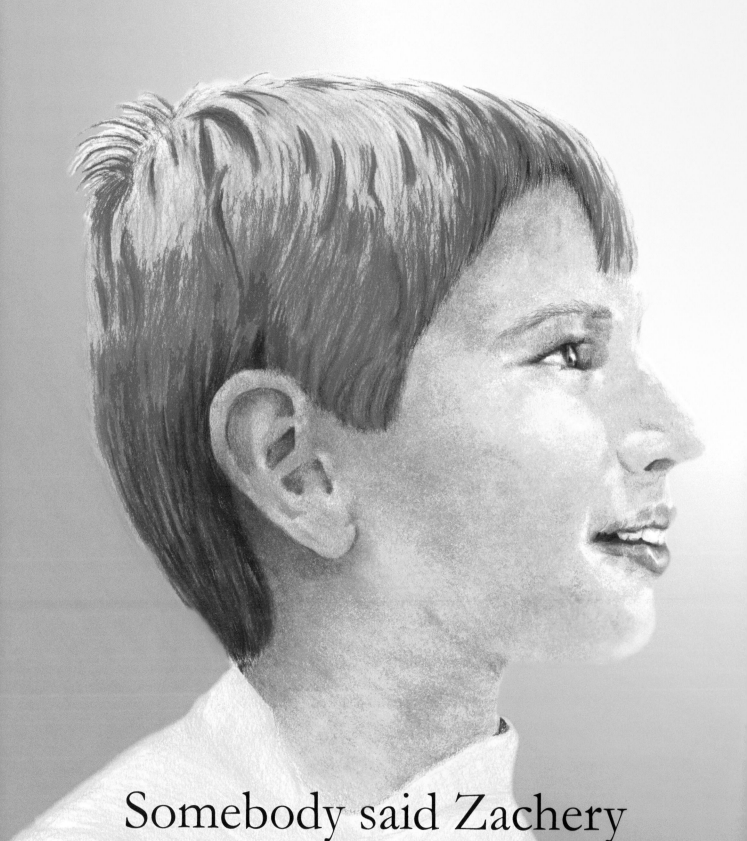

Somebody said Zachery
doesn't look people in the eyes.

But Gracie doesn't care.

SOMEBODY SAID ZACHERY HAS TO **LEAVE** THE **CLASSROOM**

SOMEBODY SAID ZACHERY **FLAPS** HIS HANDS

SOMEBODY SAID ZACHERY **BITES** HIMSELF

SOMEBODY SAID ZACHERY **WALKS ON** HIS **TIPTOES**

SOMEBODY SAID ZACHERY **CAN'T** SIT STILL AND **LISTEN**

SOMEBODY SAID ZACHERY **BANGS** HIS HEAD

SOMEBODY SAID ZACHERY **SHOUTS** WORDS

SOMEBODY SAID ZACHERY HAS **EMOTIONAL MELTDOWNS**

SOMEBODY SAID ZACHERY GIGGLES WHEN IT'S **NOT FUNNY**

SOMEBODY SAID ZACHERY **CROSSES** HIS EYES

SOMEBODY SAID ZACHERY WATCHES THINGS THAT SPIN

SOMEBODY SAID ZACHERY **DOESN'T LIKE LOUD** SOUNDS

SOMEBODY SAID ZACHERY

DOESN'T
TALK M U C H

SOMEBODY SAID ZACHERY
MAKES
FUNNY
FACES

SOMEBODY SAID
ZACHERY MAKES
HUMMING SOUNDS

SOMEBODY SAID ZACHERY
RUNS A W A Y
FROM PEOPLE

SOMEBODY SAID ZACHERY
L I N E S
UP HIS
TOYS AND
COUNTS
THEM

SOMEBODY SAID
ZACHERY
WIGGLES
HIS FINGERS

SOMEBODY SAID

ZACHERY

ONLY LIKES

THE MOVIE

CREDITS

But Gracie doesn't care.

WO

Yes, Somebody said
Zachery is different.
But Gracie doesn't care.

She just doesn't care.

Hey wait a minute.
Wait a minute.

That's not right.

GRACIE DOES CARE!

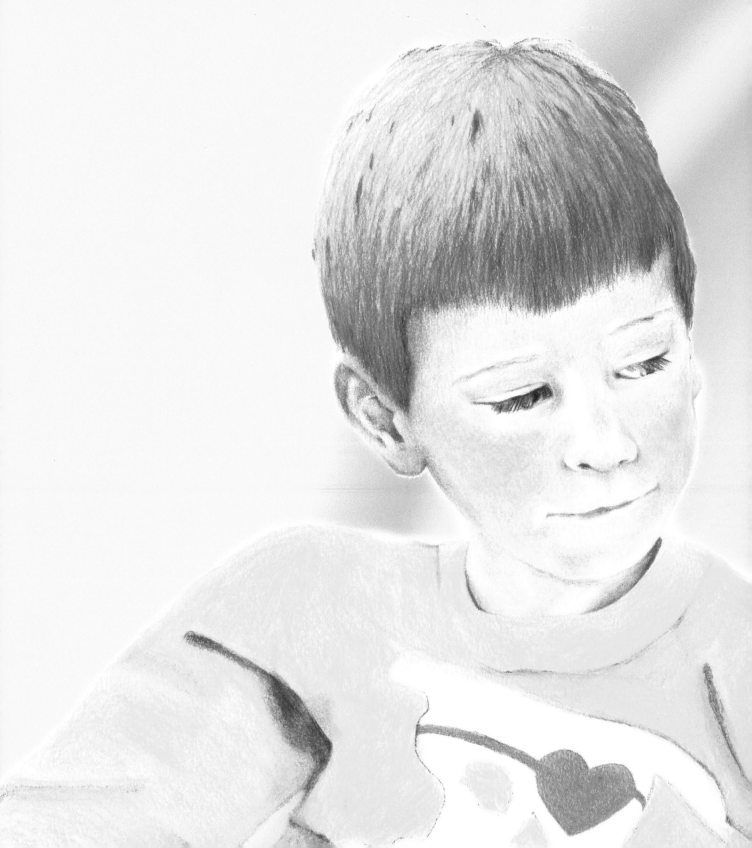

And she loves
Zachery very much.

CPSIA information can be obtained
at www.ICGtesting.com
Printed in the USA
BVHW021744291018
531545BV00003B/15/P